Grandma's Silent Auction
May
BY: Michael James

Copyright © 2020 by MICHAEL JAMES

All rights reserved.

No part of this book may be reproduced in any form or by any electronic or mechanical means, including information storage and retrieval systems, without written permission from the author, except for the use of brief quotations in a book review.

CHAPTER ONE
CIARA

I checked into my room at Seven Jewels Casino and Hotel two days ago, and haven't left it yet. I may not leave it any time soon, either. I was supposed to meet Gaetano this morning, but I didn't feel like it. It's not like he doesn't know I'm in his hotel because I'm sure he knows. If he really wanted to find me all he would have to do is come to my room and knock. Not that I would answer the door if he did. I have the right to not answer it. I can be in this room and do absolutely nothing. Who is going to stop me? I turned my cell phone off and took the phone off the hook in my room. It's just me, my heartache, and this room.

Last night I thought about checking out and leaving Vegas altogether. I even thought about going to Vibe. When I thought about leaving, I thought about all the places I could go to hide from everyone.

Jamaica sounded promising or even Hawaii. I could picture myself on the beach sipping on an island drink with those cute umbrellas in them. Maybe even have an alcoholic beverage in half a coconut. Or ten! I could really use a tan right about NOW! Now that I think of it again, it sounds like one hell of an idea. I could sneak out of here without being noticed, right? If I don't check out of the room the owner may not even realize I'm gone. Sounds like the best plan I've come up within the last few months. I leap from the bed to get my cell phone. I am going to have to turn it on if I want to book a flight.

I get my phone and come back to the bed. I hold it while I stare at it. I can't turn this stupid thing on. If I do, Grams might track it or something. I think for a second. Maybe I can't pull this off. Then I smile, hell ya, I can do this. I jump from the bed again. This time, I get my ass in the shower. I do have a way of doing this. I'm going to outsmart them all. Jamaica here I come!

I step out of the elevator dressed casually for the day. I have my purse and a few things I need to get the hell out of here. I scan the open area and see if

Gaetano is anywhere to be seen. I don't see him lingering around, so I go to the front desk and ask to use the phone.

The clerk is the same guy who checked me in two days ago. *"Is there something wrong with the phone in your room?"*

"No, but as you can see, I'm not in my room."

"Oh, sorry, I didn't mean that. I've been trying to connect a call and it's busy."

"Oh yeah, I knocked it off the hook and didn't realize it." He gets the phone and sets it on the desk. *"Thanks."* I watch him walk to the other end of the counter. He too makes a call. Now that he's busy, I call the airline to book a flight.

I hang up when I am done and simply walk right out of the hotel without any problems until the doorman stops me. I hold my breath for a second.

"Do you need the car to take you somewhere, ma'am?"

I think about it for a whole two seconds. *"I don't. I am just going for a walk."* He gives me a nod, then I start to walk away. I go down the block and once I round the corner, I flag down a cab. Nice try on finding out where I am going, Gaetano. I thought too long and too hard to let you mess this up.

My flight leaves in two hours. I have some time to

kill, but I have the driver take me right to the airport. I can go to the gift shop or something to pass the time. I just might see if they have a lounge and sip on a drink as I wait. It doesn't much matter what I do as long as I get on that plane without someone stopping me.

I fastened my seatbelt and I wish I would have had a couple more alcoholic beverages while I waited. One clearly wasn't enough. I am in panic mode. This is the worst it's ever been. I just need this plane to get into the air before I get off it. I don't understand why it is happening this badly. It's not like it's my first time flying. I've done this many times in my life. I safely make it to my destination every time. It should get easier, not tougher.

An older lady sits next to me. I lean to my right to put some space between us. I am not in a chatty mood and I hope she isn't either. I open my purse and get out my earbuds and mp3 player. I am so glad I brought it with me when I left home. I turned my playlist on and rested my head on the headrest. I try my hardest to tune out everything. In just under six hours, I'll be in Jamaica. I sure hope it's nothing but warmth, sunshine, clear water, and lots of drinks!

The stewardess is passing out snacks and drinks. She offered me something but I passed. No alcohol in it, I don't need it.

I hear the announcement that we are in the air. I feel the rush of panic disappearing. I can breathe again. I open my eyes to glance at the lady next to me. I see her talking to a man on the other side of her. I was so into my playlist that I hadn't noticed the seat was filled. I see them looking at a pamphlet. I take out my earbuds.

"Have you been to Jamaica before?"

"No, we haven't. It's our fifth anniversary and we thought what the hell let's take the honeymoon we never had."

"Aww, how nice. Happy Anniversary."

"Thank you! How about you, have you been before?"

"Nope! This was a last-minute plan. I don't even know where I'm staying once I get there."

"That's a spontaneous move. I like it."

Her husband hands me the pamphlet. Thank you, sir, it's just what I wanted. *"We did our research, this place has everything you will want."* I start looking it over. I think he's right. I give it back to him. *"Keep it, we have a spare."*

"Thank you."

I butt my nose out of their business and put my earbuds back in. I get lost in thought, I wondered what Kaiden would do to me if it were him I vanished on. I squeeze my legs together just thinking about the punishment that would unravel. God, what I would do to have his hands on me right now. I really need to stop thinking about it. My panties are wet enough.

CHAPTER TWO
CIARA

I settled into a very nice resort, thanks to the lovely couple on the plane. I have a room with a view of the aqua-blue water. I literally step outside the sliding glass door onto the white sand. I hear the water is crystal clear when you get up close to it. I can't wait to check it out for myself. However, I can't do that right now because I need clothing. I left everything back in Vegas in my room. So, the first thing I must do is go shopping. Buying a bathing suit is top on my list.

I smile when I leave my room. It feels good to just be alone. I really need to unwind and forget that the pieces of my heart are split between four men. I need this time to collect myself and figure out what I am going to do going forward. I can't keep up this being tossed from one guy to the next. It isn't mentally healthy.

I giggle, maybe I need a therapist.

I already called for a ride to take me to a shopping center. It's one of the perks of choosing this place. It is nice to know I can be shuttled around since I have no idea where I am. I can just sit back, relax, and take in the sights. I think that's a real bonus as I might never make it back here. I am going to enjoy every second that I am here.

The resort's driver drops me off and tells me he'll be waiting for me when I am done. See, this is perfect! I was just going to worry about my way back when I was done. I open the Jeep's door and he tells me to take my time. He's used to waiting. I smile and thank him.

I start window-shopping at the strip mall. I haven't seen a bathing suit that I really like yet. Maybe that is judging a store by its cover, so to speak, but the best is what should be on display. I pass by five or six stores. Honestly, I'm not counting. When I see a bathing suit in the window I like, I go inside and start looking for the exact same one. It is white and basically a two-piece bikini. There are straps that crisscross a few different times on the stomach and the back in the middle. I am happy when I find it on the rack. I frown when they don't have my size. I do, however, find it in red. I hold it under my arm as I keep browsing at the other suits. I eventually found a white one in a different style and one in mint green. I am on vacation; I'll buy all three. As I am going to the counter to cash out, I see a really adorable romper. It's a lightweight material and it's perfect to wear out to dinner.

When I finally reach the checkout, the girl asks me if I saw the wrap skirts. I shook my head no. She took it upon herself to show me. I love how she brought me, white, pink, and mint green. They are cute to wear to the pool or beach. So, she got a bigger sale. I carry my bag out and do some window shopping. I see my driver pull up and he asks if I'd like to put my bags in the Jeep. I don't have to carry bags from store to store, this spontaneous trip just keeps getting better and better. Why haven't I ever treated myself like this before?

I shopped for hours and now I have enough clothes to last me for as long as I want to stay. By the time these ten months are up, I am going to need a bigger closet. I already had too many clothes. I might have to do some serious cleaning out and donate a bunch to the local homeless shelter for women. No need to have a bunch of clothes I am never going to wear when there are ladies in need.

I took a quick shower to freshen up. I am about to head out to get a bite to eat. I am just going to stick around the resort. I saw about ten huts earlier scattered around the resort. I was told when I checked in that each one offers food and beverage. I might just stick to the closest one to my room, but we'll see. I can do whatever I want.

I use the front door instead of the sliding glass door, opposite the room. I take the paved walkway and breathe in the fresh salty air. I must say, it smells so good. It has a relaxing effect. Come to think of it, I feel a bunch of weight lifted off my shoulders. I feel much lighter. I know being here has helped that. But, I also know it has to do with the fact that I'm not thinking about the men I've been with. I have completely blocked them from my mind.

I take a gander at the first hut. It seems a little too crowded for me. I keep taking the paved sidewalk to the next one. As I walk alone, I see many couples. There are a few groups of people, probably friends hanging out. I seem to be the lone wolf. That is by choice so it doesn't bother me.

I go to the second hut and sit at the bar. It is only me and a couple here. I see the menu propped up next to a napkin holder, so I get to have a look. The bartender comes to me and gives me a warm welcome.

"Hello there, sweetie, my name is Erica Cunningham, I will be your upbeat bartender tonight. What can I get you to drink?"

"I'm not sure. Surprise me, but make it fruity."

"Alrighty!"

I look over the menu and everything sounds so good. I can't decide what I want.

"One Rum Punch!" She smiles, setting the glass down in front of me.

"Wow!" Is all I can manage to say. It looks appetizing and almost too pretty to drink. I want fruity and it sure does look fruity. *"Thank you, Erica."*

"Are you going to be ordering?"

"Yes, but I don't know what to get."

"I can hook a girl up if you need me to."

"I say go for it."

"Great! I'll put your surprise dinner in right away. It will go well with that drink."

She is super friendly. I take a sip of my drink. She definitely can make a delicious drink.

I look toward the couple. I sigh when I see him

feed her a piece of chocolate covered pineapple. I think back to when Malcolm took me to that fondue place. That was such a special moment. I pick up my drink and take a large sip. Nope not going there. I'm not going to let these men cloud my thoughts. I am here to cleanse.

I am not sitting here for more than ten minutes and my food is brought to me. Erica told me it's jerk pork. It looks wonderful and I can't wait to dig my teeth in. It's been a while since I have eaten anything. I skipped breakfast and lunch today. I didn't even eat dinner last night.

I take a bite and oh my, it's so good! My mouth practically waters for more. I give the bartender a thumbs up when she glances at me from across the bar. I ignore whatever else is going on around me and devour my dinner. I am loving Jamaica.

CHAPTER THREE
GAETANO

I wasn't in the lobby when Ciara checked-in, but I was in my office watching the monitors. She was a day early. I wasn't about to overstep and go out to welcome her. Hell, I was unsure if I was going to meet her at all. Thanks to the tabloids, I know who she dated last and I really don't like it. When I saw her here a month ago, I desperately wanted to interact with her. Her beauty is stunning. She literally took my breath away. If I had known why she was here in Vegas, or should I say, whom she was here to date, I might have stolen my twin's identity. I would have been first to date her and not have been his competition - he would have been mine.

The relationship between Kaiden and me is difficult. It's more of a relationship of hate than anything else. We may be twins, but we are not even close to being friends as twins should be. We haven't found that brotherly bond. I don't know about him, but it bothered me at first that I knew nothing about him. I wanted to get to know him. I thought he wanted to get to know me, as well. It wasn't easy learning my father lied to me for twenty-one years of my life. I'm sure it wasn't easy for him knowing his mother lied to him either. That's just the thing that keeps us from knowing each other. My father isn't his father and his mother isn't my mother. I grew up with our father and apparently my stepmother, whom I believed was my biological mother - that's the lie he told me. I lived a luxurious lifestyle. All Kaiden had was his mother. No father figure, and living dirt poor. We are two very different people. Kaiden and I tried to get to know each other the first few months of finding out about one another. I think he has a chip on his shoulder. Kaiden thinks I am a silver spoon child. We just couldn't find common ground. It is almost as if we are in a competition with each other of who can be the better man.

I set my coffee down. My words hit me hard. I get up from my desk and pace the carpeted floor. '*Better man*' keeps going through my mind. Do I want to be better than he is to Ciara? I probably could be. Is there a silent code between us even if we don't have a relationship? I didn't bid to date her just to let my brother end up with her, right?

I glance at the wall clock. I was supposed to meet her in the lobby half an hour ago. I wonder if she even showed. I could check the cameras, or just call the front desk. For some reason, I am hesitant. Thinking about it is giving me a headache.

I've been in my office for the last two hours. I'm not going to lie. I watched the video footage and I called the front desk. Ciara hasn't been seen. I phoned her room, worried something might have happened to her. All I have gotten is a busy signal every time I have tried. I thought about going up and knocking on her door. I doubt she'd answer, though. The girl hasn't even as so much as ordered room service. I thought about the possibility that she snuck out during the night. But, she hasn't checked out so I don't think that was the case. Just to make sure, I went further back in the tapes to see. No sight of Ciara since she checked in.

I try to busy myself to keep my mind off Ciara. The harder I try, the more she clouds my mind. I question if I want to know this girl because Kaiden did or is it because I think she's beautiful. When my father told me about the silent auction, I saw her picture. I thought to myself what do I have to lose. The money spent on the bid was nothing. Money is no object for me. I have enough for four lifetimes. Ninety grand wouldn't make me lose sleep over it. I did it because I have absolutely nothing to lose. Who knows maybe I get a relationship out of it. Hell, maybe she could be the one to fill my bed at night for more than a one-night stand. That's all I ever do. Most women I met want the owner of the casino and hotel, not the guy who I really am. I'm fine with how I've lived my life this far. I personally don't want a relationship with someone who doesn't appreciate me as a person instead of a dollar sign. Am I looking for love? I don't really know that I am at this point in my life. The casino and hotel take up most of the hours of my day.

I put the word out to my employees that I want to know right away if any of them see Ciara. Regardless if we do this relationship thing for the next month or not, I need to know the girl is okay. I'm not a total cold-hearted prick.

I am about ready to make my rounds on the gaming floor. I can't avoid my business just to sit here and worry about Ciara. This place is my first love. I get as far as my office door in my penthouse when my phone rings. Any other time, I might choose to not answer it. But considering I asked my employees to do something for me, I best pick it up. Hell, for all I know it could be Ciara herself.

"Gaetano Stagnitto."

"Gaetano, this is Millie Verbank. I've been trying to get a hold of my granddaughter for two days. Did you meet her today?"

"Hello, Millie. I'm afraid to say, she didn't show. Every time I try to call her I, too, get a busy signal."

"Can you please have her contact me as soon as you meet her! It's extremely important."

"Would you like me to go to her room? I was going to give her the day before I went there."

"I would really appreciate it."

I look at the receiver - goodbye to you as well!

Rudeness pisses me off. I'll only go to her room because something in her voice told me whatever she needs Ciara for does sound important. I'll make my rounds before I go to her room. Half an hour shouldn't change the importance.

CHAPTER FOUR
CLARA

I slept in today after having one too many drinks last night. After I ate my dinner at one of the huts, I stayed a little bit longer while I sipped on another drink. After that, I ventured to a couple more huts and had a few more drinks. By the time I made it back to my room, I was feeling no pain. I changed my clothes, then crawled into bed and fell right to sleep. For it being a night out by myself, I had a great time. It didn't bother me once that I didn't have a friend such as Porter with me or one of the guys I've been dating. I never did this dining alone thing before, it wasn't as bad as I always pictured.

My stomach is a little queasy, but I am dressed to go lay out by the pool. I am wearing the pink swimsuit I bought yesterday. I am pleased with how it fits. It is a little more revealing than my normal bathing suit would be, but I'm thinking outside the box. Anything I've done in the past twenty-four hours has been by far outside my comfort zone. I am kind of liking this carefree approach. I feel less stressed. That is a bonus in my book. Even before Grams set me up, I was always feeling some sort of stress. I see now how I was overworking myself. I didn't go out to dinner or clubbing unless Porter tagged along. I was in a bad relationship with Hunter and I didn't realize how much stress that caused me. I am pleased with the choice I made to come here. I have zero regrets. Grams can give Gaetano his money back. I am not going back to date him. I haven't decided what I'm going to do about Kaiden, Hawk, Malcolm, and Warrick. I just might not make a decision on that any time soon. One thing is for sure, I'm not dating Kaiden's brother. I don't know for sure if Grams knows they are twins or not - I hope she doesn't, but either way, I am putting my foot down.

As I am heading to the pool, I see a family. My heart sinks a little. If Warrick and Shay we're here, we might look just as they do… a happy little family on vacation. *Nope, don't go there Ciara. Put them out of your mind right now.*

I settle on a lounge chair. I am applying sunblock when a waiter comes over and asks if I need a drink.

My stomach is screaming, don't do it, my brain, on the other hand, says bite the dog where it bit you. I ordered a Rum punch.

I settle into the chaise lounge and do a little people watching while I wait for my drink. It's early afternoon and the pool area isn't as packed as I saw it yesterday. Which is fine. If it is too crowded I may leave. I want to just lay here and relax and not be disturbed.

The waiter hands me my drink then I place it on the table. I sign the receipt for the drink to be charged to my room. I then sit back and pick up my cocktail. I have my first sip. A little sip. I smile when it doesn't affect me in a bad way. My fingers are crossed that this slight hangover won't last long.

I've been soaking up the sun for the last two hours. I finished my cocktail and ordered another one. This time, I got sex on the beach. Just saying the name makes me think of sex. All the incredible sex I had with Kaiden. I had to put that out of my mind quickly. I rolled over to get sun on my back. I am not going to lay here much longer as I don't want to burn my second day here. I didn't come here to be holed up in my room.

I feel hot. Sweaty hot. Please tell me I didn't fall asleep in the sun. I hear a man close by placing a drink order. I pick my head up to see just how close the voice really is. All I see is the waiter's ass. I don't bother waiting to see who is right next to me. I am going to give it five minutes then I am casually going to leave. I could use a dip in the pool to cool off. I might do that before leaving.

"I hope you put sunscreen on your back."

Shit, now this person wants to chit chat! I don't want to strike up a conversation with any man. I pick my head up and look his way. *"Kaiden?"*

"Nope, my name is - ."

"Gaetano Stagnitto!"

"Ahh, he did tell you about me."

I get up. *"How did you do it?"*

"Do what?"

"Don't play coy with me. You know damn well what I mean."

"You missed our meeting. I asked the front desk to let me know if they saw you."

"That isn't how you figured out I left."

"I might have listened to the call you made?"

"That is a violation of privacy."

"I did it with good reason."

"Whatever." I stand. I have to get away from this asshole and his stupid grin.

I drop my sunglasses on the lounge, then I go to the pool and dive in. Now I just need him to get the hint and leave me alone. I swim and gosh does the water feel good. My core was hotter than I thought. I peeked a few times and Gaetano didn't get my hint. He watched me with a careful eye. Jerk! The only way I'm going to get away from him is to go to my room. Which, I'm sure he knows where it is. How he found me at this resort is beyond me. I sure as hell didn't know where I was staying until I arrived.

I get out of the pool. I ring my hair out as I go to where I was sitting. His eyes travel over every inch of my body.

"You can stop gawking at me."

"Sweetheart, with a suit that is as revealing as yours is, every man here has his eyes on you. Probably even the ladies. I happen to like the color pink suddenly."

I look down. My nipples are showing right through.

I can only imagine what else can be seen. I reach for my towel to hide. I changed my mind. I make a stance. Might as well show him what he's not getting.

"Get a good look now, it's as close to naked as you'll see my body." I wink. *"The only time, as well."*

He smiles. Damn him it's just how Kaiden smiles. I grab my towel to cover up. Kaiden wouldn't like his brother's eyes on me this way.

"That's a shame you hide behind a towel. But don't worry, I'll have that image in my mind for some time." He returns my wink.

"You can go back to your casino and hotel. I have no desire to date Kaiden's twin."

He rises off his chaise lounge. He is literally in my space. *"I see we are playing hard to get. It's been awhile since I've chased someone for a thrill. Wait until the tabloids catch us together. It will drive Kaiden crazy."* I reach up to slap him. He catches my arm by the wrist before I make contact. *"Careful, my punishments might be more intense then what my brother gives."*

"Go to hell, Gaetano."

I start to walk away. *"Ciara, you might need this."* I look back to see what he has. *"Millie really needs to speak with you. I don't know her, but it sounded very important."*

"You went into my room?"

"Yes, only to see if you had your phone. I'm serious, she had sadness in her voice. I charged it on the way here."

I take my phone from him. *"Don't follow me."*

I get into my room. I toss my phone on the bed. I'm so irritated with him. First, he violated my privacy on the phone, then went into my room. He is an asshole in my mind. He's someone I don't want to know at all. As for Grams, I sure hope that isn't a trap. I don't want to listen to her bitch at me about Jacquelyn or skipping out on Gaetano. So much for my freedom!

CHAPTER FIVE
GAETANO

I had a hard time finding Ciara once I landed in Jamaica early this morning. By early morning, I am talking at four a.m., early. Thanks to my computer geek friend, Doug, he made it much easier for me. Within an hour of arriving, I knew where she was staying. She had an entire day here to think she got away. I wasn't going to waste another day of our month together. She's not getting away. I don't mind playing a little game of chase. I sort of find it exciting.

Originally I chased after Ciara because of Millie's phone call. On the flight, I decided that I am going to try to get to know her. She is a beautiful girl and I find that I am curious - curious about what makes her tick. I am really curious as to why she was auctioned off like an item. Shouldn't a girl with a successful business, money in the bank, and sexy as hell, already have been taken off the market, not being put on the market? I would not ever let my family do this to me - ever!

I was walking around, getting a feel for the resort when I saw Ciara. She got my attention as she did so many other men. She made herself comfortable at the pool. I watched as she applied sunscreen. I had to look away as I didn't care to get an erection in public. Her bathing suit alone is enough to excite any man. After she settled back to get some sun, I didn't stick around. I wanted to keep scoping out the place and get ideas on things to do here.

I returned to the pool an hour later. I sat right next to her and She didn't even notice. That was when I realized she was sleeping. I sure hope she has sunblock on her back. She may regret falling asleep in the sun, especially in this sun that she isn't used to. I was ordering a drink when I saw her foot move. I couldn't see her face as the waiter was in the way. I wanted to give him a swift kick to move out of the way. I was happy when he finally moved.

It looked as if maybe she didn't wake after all. I spoke to her, and if she didn't wake before, she did now. It bothered me more than I wanted when she called me Kaiden. I can only hope the sun glare or the sleep in her eyes caused that. Yes, Kaiden is my twin. It really is hard to tell us apart, but there are a few slight differences between us. I have a little bit more graying to my hair. Kaiden is an inch shorter than I am. Other than that, you can't tell us apart. Hell, we both even wear a tight beard and have the same haircut. I don't know how many times I've been called by his name. Ciara doing it shouldn't be any different, but it was. It bothered me. I didn't like it at all. At least she did know my name. I tried to be cool about her missing our meeting, but she has sass. I don't think she liked me listening to her conversation or that I went into her room. I don't see it as intruding, we are supposed to be dating.

The little bickering between us was a little comical to me until she got out of the pool. I played it off as a joke, but I didn't like her suit to be so revealing. I was okay with it for my eyes. However, she was mine to date and her body isn't for the prying eyes that were on her. Although I was relieved when she covered up, I was also disappointed. Her body is fucking incredible. I have to admit I was more disappointed when she left. She isn't going to get far without me knowing. My room is right next door to hers.

It is about time for dinner. I got dressed in a nice pair of shorts and a short-sleeved dress shirt. I have been sitting outside the sliding door in a patio chair for a little while. I've been enjoying the fresh salty air while having a tropical mixed drink. I figure I will give Ciara a half an hour to emerge from her room. If she doesn't, I have no problem knocking on her door. The girl has to eat, and I am going to make sure it is with me. I didn't come all this way to dine alone or vacation alone now that I decided I'm staying put. I want my chance to know her and for her to know me. I am more than Kaiden's look-a-like. I have a lot to offer Ciara. There is more to my life than my Casino and Hotel. I have an entire family that would welcome her into their lives if she would let them. I know Ciara only has her grandmother. I can give her holidays, birthdays, and family BBQs, stuff that she has never had. I think she would like to be part of a close-knit family. She won't know what she is missing until she allows me to show her who I am. I am more than ever determined to make my presence known. I am not going to give up without a fight. When I want something, I go for it. I never hold back. I refuse to do that now because Kaiden got to her first. Fuck the brother code. Just because we share the same DNA doesn't make us real brothers.

I hear the sliding of her glass door. I peek through the lattice fencing dividing us. She looks beautiful as always. She has on this cute, flowy sundress. When she turns around to close her door, I can see the white marks from where her swimsuit was. The poor girl's back is red. She got burnt. I could kick myself in the ass for not waking her when I saw that she was asleep in the hot sun. When I get a good look at her face, I sit up straighter. Has she been crying? I move to the edge of my seat when she begins to walk in the sand toward the common area of the resort. I open my mouth to say her name, but I pause. Maybe I should give her some peace. I don't know the details of why she has been crying. I really don't care to upset her even more. I rub my chin, what is the right thing to do here? Chase after the woman I want to know or leave her be for the time being? This is why I don't do relationships, they are a pain in the ass to figure out.

CHAPTER SIX
CIARA

I wasn't going to go out to the huts tonight for dinner. I was just going to stay in. I called Grams back once I got to my room. What she told me really upset me. It floored me really. My heart instantly was filled with sadness. Then anger set in, I was so pissed at myself for being so damn selfish by shutting everyone I know out. Lesson learned I won't ever leave my phone turned off for days ever again. I was so careless. I feel horrible about it. I feel even worse about the news she told me. I am still upset about it and now it is my turn to wait with my stomach in knots.

I got dressed to venture out only because I need to search for Gaetano. It had nothing to do with wanting to eat. I need to find him so that I can thank him for bringing me my phone. He didn't have to go out of his way to do that and he did. I owe him a huge thank you.

I bypass the first hut as I did last night and go to the next one. I have a seat at the quaint little bar. The same girl, Erica comes to wait on me. I ordered a fruit punch without alcohol. I don't bother to look at the menu this time. As I said, I didn't come out to eat. I have no appetite.

I look around to see if Gaetano might be here. I am disappointed when he isn't here. I might have to keep moving. I cross my fingers he didn't get on a plane and jet his ass back to Vegas. It would be less complicated if he wasn't still here, though.

I sign for my drink and charge it to my room. I twirl in my seat.

"Evening."

"Hey, I was just…" I pause and stare at him for too long. He raises his eyebrow.

"Mind if I sit."

"Yes."

"Yes, you do mind?"

I find my thoughts. His smile really gets to me. *"No, please have a seat. I was actually looking for you."*

"Really? That's a switch from this afternoon."

"I know. I need to thank you for bringing my

phone to me. That call from Grams was very important."

"Good. You are welcome." He sits next to me then reaches out a hand. I put mine in his. I smile when he kisses my hand. *"Hi, Ciara, I'm Gaetano Stagnitto."*

"Hello, Gaetano."

"Fresh start?"

"I'd like that."

"How about I buy you some dinner?"

"Okay," I say even though I'm not really hungry.

"What are you drinking? It looks good."

I giggle. *"Fruit punch without alcohol in it."*

"Sounds wonderful."

He waves a hand in the air and Erica comes right over. He does get the same drink I have, then asks for menus. She glances at me with a look of approval at my choice of company. I Nonchalantly shrug my shoulders. She grins. I start looking over the items. I just want something light.

"See anything you like? We can go elsewhere if you don't."

"I think I'll just go with jerk chicken salad." I set the menu down. *"How about you?"*

"I'll have what you are having."

I smile because I'm not used to a guy getting the

same thing as I do. Generally, it's the other way around. It's also nice that he didn't order anything extra just because I may not like what I got.

"How long are you staying?"

"Not sure yet, it does depend on one thing."

"What's that?"

"How long are you staying?"

"I see. I'm not really sure. It could be tonight or it could be a week from now."

"Tonight? Why rush out of this beautiful place when you just got here."

I am just about to answer him when my phone rings. I look at it and the knots in my stomach double. I excuse myself to take the call.

"Hello."

"Hey, baby."

"Oh, my God, Hawk are you alright?"

"I'm feeling no pain." I frown when I hear him slurring his words. *"My car is not so good."*

"I heard. A car can be replaced, you can't be."

"Damn it was a fast one though."

"Are you really okay? I saw how bad your wreck was."

"I feel…"

"Hawk?"

"I'm high." He laughs. *"Ouch. Don't laugh. It hurts to laugh."*

"What are your injuries? Who is with you?"

"Here talk to Carl."

"No, I don't want…"

"Hi, Ciara. Hawk is a little doped up."

"Is he going to be alright?"

"He will be once he heals. I'm sure he'll be a joy to deal with until then."

"Carl," I say loudly, *"what are his injuries?"*

"Broken leg and a few cracked ribs."

Tears well up in my eyes. I wish I were with him. I want to hug him. *"Can you put him back on the phone? Please."*

"Hawk Evans! Who is this?"

"Ciara!"

"Hey, baby. I miss you."

"I miss you, too."

"I'm really tired. Call me tomorrow. I love you."

I look at the phone. *"Love you,"* I say to a dead connection.

I wipe my eyes. I feel somewhat better now that I heard his voice. I do, however, wish I could be with him right now.

I take my seat next to Gaetano. He touches my

bare back. I want to scream. *"You need to put something on that. It's very warm to the touch."*

"I will later."

Our meals arrived, and I choked down the food I didn't want. It tastes good, but my stomach has been in knots since calling Grams. She called to tell me Hawk wrecked his car in practice yesterday. She didn't want me to hear it on the news. As soon as we hung up, I googled it. I thought I was going to get sick when I saw the car. There was no information on his condition. I called his number, and this is the first I heard back from him. I am relieved he is going to be fine. It doesn't make it any easier knowing I'm not there for him. When you love someone, you should be there next to them.

"Your recommendation was superb."

"Tomorrow you should try the jerk pork. It's really good."

"I will do that if we are still here." I nod my head. *"Is everything alright with the call you got?"*

"Yeah, I think so."

"I don't want this night to end, but you look exhausted. I really think you need to put cream or something on your back."

"I am tired. I don't really have anything to put on my back. I'm sure it will be fine by morning."

"How about I walk you to your room and then I get cream that I brought with me. I'll even put it on for you." My eyes go wide. *"The back is tough to reach."*

"Okay, but nothing else," I make very clear to him

He uses his arm and hand to gesture for me to lead the way. Gaetano seems like a nice guy. Too bad for him he looks like someone else. A person that I love. I don't see how I can look past that.

We get to my room and I am at the front door when he tells me his room is right next to mine. Coincidence, I think not. I am too exhausted to care. I am sure it was done on purpose and see no reason to bring it up.

I go inside and leave the door open. I set my purse on the table as I passed through the room. I get to the sliding doors and open them, then pull the screen door closed. It's nice out and I want the fresh air in the room. I rub my arms as I get chills. I go to where there's a mirror mounted on the wall above the dresser. I turn so that I can see my back. I am really sunburnt. It definitely is worse than I thought.

"Here, let me."

I twist back to face the mirror. I watch him apply cream of some kind. It is cool against my skin. I put my head down and close my eyes. I can't look at Gaetano touching me. I pick my head back up. Closing my eyes wasn't a good idea, either. I stare at Gaetano in the mirror. I see graying on top in his hair that Kaiden doesn't have. It looks good on him. There is something else that seems different but I can't figure it out.

I gasp when Gaetano gets down to his knees and applies cream to the backs of my legs. He starts at my calf and works his way to my thigh. I hold my breath as his hand inches higher. He stops just under my ass cheek. I let out the breath I was holding.

"There. I think I got all the hard to reach places."

"Thank you."

"You are welcome." He reaches in his pocket and then hands me a couple of pills. *"Benadryl. It will help when it starts to itch. Probably help you sleep, too. The amount of sun you got is draining. Make sure you drink plenty of fluids."*

"Thank you, Dr. Stagnitto."

He laughs. *"Far from it. I may have had a burn or two."*

We look at each other for a moment. *"Seriously, thank you for the cream. I want to say thank you again for bringing me my phone. It means a lot to me. It was very important. I was mad that you went through my things and followed me, but I'm not anymore."*

"You don't need to thank me. It was my way of showing you I want the chance to know you." He reaches up and touches my cheek. *"Get some rest. I'll see you in the morning."*

We say goodnight and he leaves. I take the pills he gave me with some water. I strip out of my clothes and slip under the light blanket. Even though I have chills, my skin is on fire.

CHAPTER SEVEN
GAETANO

I didn't go right to sleep when I left Ciara's room. Hell, I didn't even go back to my room. I went for a walk around the resort to cool off. After having my hands on Ciara's body, I was a little worked up, especially getting so close to her great ass. Her ass is very spankable. It was too damn tempting. There was no way I was going near it to put cream on it. Although I'm sure it needed it. I hope she did it herself. I know damn well her suit barely covered her cheeks. Even thinking about how perfect her ass is and how close I was to touching it, my manhood started to get hard while walking. I needed to get her off my mind if I didn't want to end up pleasuring myself. That still wasn't out of the question once I returned to my room.

I walked around for quite some time before going

back to my room. Luckily by the time I did make it back there I was tired enough to call it a night. Ciara's ass was no longer in the front of my mind. She was. I crawled into bed and thought of a few things we could do together. I am hoping she'll take me up on my offer. I am also hoping that Hawk Evans doesn't keep interrupting my time with her. I saw her screen before she answered. I already knew who he was from the tabloids. Out of curiosity, I googled him. I found out the reason she was so thankful I brought her phone. I am the fifth guy she's dating in the ten-month long auction thing. I don't like it. The not knowing how far her feelings go for the other guys is unnerving. What if I am just wasting my time on a woman who is already in love with someone else. It's never far from my mind, that someone may be my twin. Falling in love may be a long shot. I went to sleep last with the questioning thought, is it worth it?

I woke this morning without the answer to my question from the night before. As I was having my morning coffee outside my door, it became clear to me that I had to find a way to get inside her head on this whole dating game. I had to know just how serious she is taking it. The main thing I have to find out is whether she is in love with the previous men. This going back and forth in my head, if I really want to do this or not, needs to end. It's either we try this relationship thing or we part ways. I'm not into playing games unless it's gambling.

I called for room service. When it arrived at my room, I took it over to Ciara's back door. I set up her table for two. It was nice, but it was missing something. Then I remember seeing some beautiful flowers along the walkway. I didn't want to be greedy, so I only picked one. I set it on her plate. Pleased with my romantic breakfast table, I knocked on her door. I clearly woke her. She got out of bed without thinking and got the bathrobe from the bathroom. I couldn't look away as a gentleman should do. Nope, I watched her naked body walking to the bathroom. Christ, I was getting hard.

"Good morning," I said when she came to the screen door.

She yawns. *"Morning."* She looks at me through half hooded eyes. *"What time is it?"*

"Seven."

"In the morning?"

I laugh. *"Yes.*

"Ugh, it's too early." She turns to head back to her bed.

"I ordered you some breakfast." Her head

dropped and her shoulders slumped. *"I take it you're not a morning person?"*

"You guessed right."

I knew I had to keep talking or my entire breakfast would be wasted. *"Coffee is hot. I got that fruit punch you like. I'm sure your body would love some fluids."*

She faces me. She rubs her eyes. *"If we are doing this whole get to know each other thing, the first thing to make me happy is to let me sleep until at least nine."*

"Great, I'll remember that for tomorrow."

I want to laugh when she rolls her eyes. I also want to rip her robe off and spank her bare ass. It would sting more with the redness from yesterday's sun. *"You should eat. I might have made plans for us today."*

Ciara looks down at the covered plate. She picks up the flower next to it and brings it to her nose. She inhales the flowery scent. She then twirls it around between her fingers as if she's thinking. I wish I could read her mind. I watch as she takes another sniff before placing it on the table. Suddenly she lifts the cover off her plate. Her eyes grow wide. I think I might have missed the opportunity to impress her. With not knowing what kind of food she enjoys, I went with something I believe most women like - chocolate.

"I love chocolate chip pancakes."

Relief overcomes me. I realize I am happy to get something right. I lift the dome off mine. *"One of my favorite breakfast meals. I like to spread jam on them instead of syrup."*

"Sounds good."

Putting my hand over my chest, expressing my shock. *"Don't tell me you have never tried it that way."*

"There's a first time for everything, right?"

"Right."

Ciara watches me spread the strawberry jam over the top of my pancakes. I don't wait for her to do the same. Cutting off a piece, I bring my fork to her mouth. She takes the bite I'm offering. She moans with satisfaction. I sold her on my style of pancakes.

We walk down to the beach to where there are private tents set up. I love her expressions. It's as if nobody has taken the time to spoil this woman. She seems surprised by nice gestures. I for one love watching her smile get wider. It's even better knowing I put it there.

"What is this?"

"Couples massage while taking in the fresh air for a total relaxation experience."

"You are full of surprises this morning."

"Hmm and to think it is only the morning." I wink and give her a smile.

"That sounds a little devilish, Mr. Stagnitto."

I don't reply as our massage therapists come to take us inside. I am looking forward to this as much as Ciara is. I can get a massage any day of the week, but it lacks this atmosphere.

We both get changed into bathrobes and lay on the tables and face each other. The ladies start applying hot coconut oil on our backs. Ciara closes her eyes as fingers start to knead and work her muscles. I have to stop watching. All I can think about is it being my hands instead, applying the hot oil. Or hell even hot wax. The more time I am spending with her the more I want to take this girl to bed. There are so many things I want to do to her body. Giving her pleasure that is beyond a normal sex life, is one of them. I know my brother is a Dom. I am too. I kind of wonder if he even told her. When the time comes to lay her down in my bed, I need to know if she enjoyed it. I don't want to push my lifestyle choice on her if she isn't into it. I also know I can't be with anyone who isn't. I am too set in my ways.

"This is the life."

I open my eyes. There for a second, I thought she could read my mind. *"There's a spa in the hotel. I go to it at least once a week."*

"How often do you leave the hotel and casino?"

"Not as often as I should."

"You were there when I checked into your hotel a month ago."

"Yes."

"I won on that machine, by the way."

"Max bet is where it's at."

"Why didn't you tell me who you were?"

"I didn't know why you were in Vegas. I knew it wasn't for me."

"Wait, you didn't know I was in Vegas to meet Kaiden?"

"Nope, didn't know until I saw the tabloids."

"So, he has no idea I am with you?"

"No. Millie didn't give us a list of our competitors."

"Competitors," she says very softly.

That probably wasn't my best choice of words. It is honest though. We are ten guys trying to fall in love and have her love us back. There will only be one of us that she will choose to marry.

Ciara has gone quiet. I think now is the perfect time to make my exit. I get off the table, fully exposing myself. It is no big deal to me to be naked in front of a beautiful woman.

Her eyes didn't seem to mind the view. *"Are we done?"*

"I am, you are not."

"What does that mean?"

"It means, relax and enjoy the pampering today. I'll be at your door at five. I have something planned for us."

I give her a light kiss to her cheek before I make my exit. I want her to enjoy the day I planned for her, but I also want it to be five o'clock already.

I head back to my room to get changed. I am meeting a very important person for a round of golf. I am glad, too, because I need some advice.

CHAPTER EIGHT
CIARA

The lady giving me my massage tells me to roll over. I do as she asked and she begins to work the hot coconut oil into my skin. I try to relax, but my mind will not shut off. I can't stop thinking about Kaiden. I don't want him to find out I'm dating his brother by reading it in the tabloids. I know him, he isn't going to take that news very well. I would rather he hear it from me than anywhere else. As soon as I get out of the tent, I'm calling him.

I feel more relaxed now that I've made up my mind. This lady is amazing with her hands. She really gets deep into the tissue. I wouldn't be surprised if I'm not a little sore after all this treatment. No pain no gain, I guess.

"I'm all done."

I smile at the lady. When I sit up, she tells me to lay back down because I'm not done. It confused me for a second until she left and another lady came in. She announced that she'll be doing a facial on me. She asked me a bunch of questions before she got started. I was content, ready to go, but then the steaming hot towel was placed on my face. It feels like heaven. I love getting facials. I find them more relaxing than a massage. I won't be surprised if I fall asleep.

I yawn and stretch. My body is a bit stiff. Damn, am I thirsty. I look around. Shit, I did fall asleep. I get up and put my bathrobe on, then step outside. I almost want to go back into the tent. It was cooler in there. I jump when a voice comes out of nowhere.

"Feel more relaxed?"

"I do. Thank you."

"You look so much better. Now that you are awake, we must get going."

"Going? Where are we going?"

"Some more Jamaica pampering."

"I need to go to my room first."

"Of course, sweetie, you need to get dressed."

I start to go to my room. The white sand is warm already. I look back and the lady is quietly following.

I wonder where she is taking me. I want to call Kaiden right away. I want privacy while I do that. I unlock my room. Do I tell her not to come in?

I politely say, *"I'll be right out. Please have a seat and make yourself comfortable."* With the nod of her head, she sits.

I shut the door and go right for my phone. I pray he answers. Mostly, I hope this doesn't crush him.

"Ciara, I have missed your voice. I miss everything about you, really. Did you read the email I sent you?"

I whisper his name. *"Kaiden,"* I cannot get any other words out.

"What's the matter?"

"I have something to tell you."

"So you did read my email?"

"No, I haven't. I didn't even know you sent me one."

"Something is very wrong. I can hear it in your voice."

"I...," I don't want to do this. *"Do you know who I am with?"* I finally blurt out.

"No."

"When I left your place, I didn't leave Vegas. I checked into a hotel and locked myself inside for two

days, then I kind of took off to Jamaica - alone. I wanted to escape. I did not want to be with the next guy."

"It's Gaetano, isn't it?"

"Yes."

"Are you still in Jamaica?"

"Yes."

"Did he follow you?"

"Yes." Kaiden goes very quiet. I can picture him rubbing the back of his neck while he paces the room. *"I can't look at him and not see you. He is nice and seems to be ready to try a relationship with me, despite the fact I was with you. I had to personally tell you. I couldn't let it be plastered on a tabloid for you to see."*

"I almost don't know what to say. I wish I could come and get you. It already wasn't easy letting you go into another man's arms. Knowing it's my twin, makes it even harder."

"I don't know what to do. Tell me what to do."

"I wish I could, but you know I can't do that. I'll tell you this, read the email I sent you. If it means anything to you at all, I won't worry. If it means nothing, I will eventually get over it. I need you to do what is best for Ciara and nobody else. That includes me."

"I have to go."

"I'm always a phone call away whenever you need me. I'm not just saying that for today, this week, or next month. I mean it for however long you need me. I hope that is forever."

I let out the air I was holding in my lungs. I look at the screen of my phone, wishing he didn't hang up. Hearing his voice hurts. It pains him as much as it does me to be with Gaetano. If I met Gaetano first, it might feel the opposite way around.

I get changed into a pair of jean shorts and a tank top. I have no idea where that lady is taking me, so who knows if I am wearing the correct clothing or not. I really don't much care.

When I step outside. She doesn't say anything. I guess I am good to go. We get into a Jeep and she hands me an ice-cold bottle of water, telling me my body needs to drink plenty of fluids today after such an intense massage. I take the water and start drinking it. I watch the scenery as she drives us. Honestly, I'm not paying that much attention to what is around me. I'm wondering what Kaiden said in his email. I haven't taken the time to read it yet. I didn't want this lady to keep waiting for me.

We aren't in the car long before she pulls up to

this octagon building with tons of beautiful flowers all around. I don't think we've gone too far from the resort.

"Are you ready to get even more gorgeous than you already are?"

"I'm not getting plastic surgery, am I?" I laugh so that she knows I'm joking.

"None needed, sweetie."

We go inside and I see a salon chair, manicure and pedicure stations. I am going to enjoy this. *"Where would you like me?"*

"How about we do feet first? You should pick out a color you like."

I am browsing the colors. I ask, *"What is your name?"*

"Sharilyn Russell."

"It's nice to meet you. Are you from here?"

"Nope, I came on vacation and never left."

"I can see why."

I pick a color and have a seat in the pedicure chair. I don't generally like people touching my feet, but for this I think I can manage. Sharilyn fills the foot tub and leaves me be. I take out my phone to read the email Kaiden sent me.

Ciara, you haven't even left me yet and here I am already missing you. I have one more precious day to be with you. This past month has simply been amazing in every way possible. I'm not ready to give you up. I don't know that I'll ever be ready for that. This month flew by way too fast. There is so much I still want to share with you. So many words left untold. I can think of three words I want desperately to say to you. However, I am saving them. When the right time comes, I'll never stop saying those three little words that mean so much. The next six months are going to be agonizing. I long for the day to come that I am yours as much as you are mine. Take Care, Ciara. - Kaiden Marcellus.

I hold my phone to my chest. His words mean so much to me. Kaiden and I didn't say I love you to each other. Sometimes actions do speak louder than words. We have a phenomenal connection. Our chemistry is breathtaking.

I think about our conversation a little while ago. I then put my cell in my purse. When I reply to him, I want to make sure my words are pure and as truthful as possible. I am not out to hurt anyone's feelings. I don't want to be that girl who breaks hearts. Out of all the men I've been with, I feel like I want to guard Kaiden's heart.

Sharilyn sits at my feet. *"Are you ready for this?"*

I brace myself for my feet to be touched. I squint my eyes closed and peek one open. *"I think so."*

Sharilyn laughs and so do I. She strikes up a conversation. She's very good at what she does. I mean, I haven't kicked her so that is a plus. I love her tactics of getting my mind off my ticklish feet.

CHAPTER NINE
GAETANO

Today is just what I needed. Nothing like a round of golf to soothe the soul. The company I had was pretty nice, too. It was exactly what I needed. The advice was an added bonus.

I get dressed into a pair of light, black dress pants and a long-sleeved, red dress shirt and roll the sleeves a quarter of the way up. I leave a few buttons undone at the top. I then splash some aftershave on. I am ready to take Ciara out tonight for an enjoyable evening on the beach.

I knock on her door and she answers right away. She is always beautiful, but damn, how can she keep getting more stunning every time I see her?

"Wow," is all I can manage to say. She smiles and does a twirl. Her sundress flared out and I got a peek at her lean legs through the slit. *"You look lovely."*

"Thanks to you. Sharilyn is a goddess."

"I think you are the Goddess."

She slightly blushes. *"That's sweet of you to say."*

I hold out my elbow. *"I hope you like what I have planned."*

Her smile gets big. *"Not sure you can top the amazing day you already gave me, but I'm willing to find out."*

I am very pleased to know she enjoyed her day. Women should be pampered and know that they are cherished. If things keep going this good, that was just the tip of the iceberg. I plan on spoiling her and make it known that I have no problem with showering her with surprises and gifts.

We walk down to the beach and so many people have decided to come to the festivities tonight. The smell of food roasting fills the salty air. Music plays as people fill their bellies. Drinks are being consumed and everyone seems to be having a good time. Ciara and I find a place to sit at one of many large round tables and we sit down on the big, fluffy mats on top the sand. Tonight isn't about dining alone at your own table, it's about meeting and getting to know strangers. I think it's perfect. Ciara and I are practically strangers getting to know one another. We sat at a table that is more than half empty. These tables seat at least ten people. I didn't take count but it looks about right.

"This is so cool. I never thought I would be doing something like this."

"It is refreshing, isn't it."

"Thank you so much. I needed a day like this. Sharilyn kept my mind off my troubles."

"What trouble?"

"You aren't seriously asking me, are you?"

"Yes, I am. How can you have troubles in this paradise?"

"Gee, Gaetano, maybe that fact that my life got turned upside because of my grandmother."

"I see. I guess you have to ask yourself if this process is worth the outcome. You have the possibility to meet the love of your life. Yes, I'm sure you will go through difficult times, but going through troubles is how you know if a relationship is strong enough to withstand anything."

"I get what you are saying. I really do. What I meant by troubles is trying to deal with my feelings. I meet a guy, develop feelings then I have to go through a breakup, just to do it all over again. Come November I have to basically know who I love the most. It weighs heavily on my mind nonstop."

I just heard her basically confess that she has

fallen in love with the four guys before me. *"I don't know about the other guys, so I can only speak for myself. If I develop feelings for you, I too will have to go through the breakup. I will have to wait five months wondering if I'll be the one you pick. That isn't going to be easy. I can't imagine it's easy for the first guy second and so on. We are all humans putting everything on the line to be the one. We just met, but I think you are an incredible woman. If I fall in love, it won't be easy knowing you are off to be in another man's arms. I'll be questioning myself every day you are gone if I gave you enough of myself to be that guy that ends up with you. I'm sure the first four guys are already wondering."*

"I cannot wrap my head around how any of you would want to be with me in the end. Relationships happen. Sex is a big part of it. How can any of you love me knowing I might sleep with all of you. The tabloids have called me a slut, it hurts, but it's kind of true."

"When I signed up for this and put my bid in, I think we all kinda knew in the back of our minds that was a possibility. None of us are angels. We all have a sexual past and many partners. Look at Hawk Evans. He's a known player, did that bother you when you slept with him?"

"Who says I slept with him?"

"I don't know that you did. I was using that as an example."

"I slept with Kaiden. If we end up together, can you live with knowing I had sexual relations with your twin?"

"Do you think he can handle knowing if we slept together?"

"To answer your question, no it didn't bother me that Hawk was a player before me."

I like how she avoided my question. That tells me either she doesn't know the answer or doesn't want to tell me he wouldn't like it at all. Outside of this situation, I would be livid if the person I was in love with slept with my brother. But this isn't a normal dating situation.

Ciara looked very uncomfortable as our conversation turned deep. I have to rectify that. I need to see her carefree self and put her smile back on her face.

"I don't know about you, but I'm famished."

"Ugh, I thought we'd never eat."

I stand and help Ciara get up from the ground. She dusts off her ass even though the mats keep the sand off. I take her hand as we walk toward where the food is being cooked. I am looking forward to digging my teeth into the roast pig.

Ciara and I stuffed ourselves with roasted pig, roasted fruits and the best banana bread I have ever had. We had tried a coconut rum mixed with pineapple and it was pleasantly good. We have been enjoying the music and a much lighter conversation. I have another surprise tonight, but it hasn't showed up yet. I have been keeping my eye out and wondering where the hell it is.

I stand and ask Ciara to dance with me. I must keep her wanting to stay where we are at. I am sure my surprise will show, I hope that will happen soon. I am really excited about it.

I lead the way to the spot that others have used as a dance floor. I hold her close to my body as we begin to sway to the music. We are barely getting into the slow dance when the beat changes. I twirl her around and when I bring her back, I put her back to my chest. I bend my head and place a kiss on the side of her neck. She didn't seem to mind it. I twirl her again and this time, she faces me. I cup her face with one hand and kiss her. To my surprise, she kisses me back. Goddamn, this woman is getting to me. I like her. And boy do I want to introduce her to my bedroom. I want to put my hands on every inch of her body. I want to know the sounds she makes as she cums.

"You are quite the dancer, Mr. Stagnitto."

"Glad you think so. My dance instructor thought I had two left feet."

She laughs. *"Well she must have been blind."*

"No, I pretty much think I crushed her toes one too many times."

We went back to the table where we ate our dinner to get our drinks. Then we move closer to the music. We barely get settled in our new place before my surprise finally shows up. I introduce Ciara to my family. Her jaw is about on the floor. I'm not so sure she likes this surprise. She wouldn't even shake my father's hand. Shit! I might have messed up.

CHAPTER TEN
CIARA

Wow, is all I can think right now. I am in total shock that Gaetano would invite his family here. I get you should be introduced to the family during this process, but wow, we hardly know each other. I met Malcolm's and Warrick's family but that was after knowing each other better. I feel I am stuck getting to know someone who I have a very negative opinion of. I don't know his side of the story, however, I know Kaiden's and I am not impressed.

I close my mouth once I realize my jaw is on the ground. I look right at Gaetano. After that kiss we shared when we were dancing, I finally felt I could see him and not Kaiden. They kiss nothing alike. I can't do this whole relationship with him if I cannot stop wanting Gaetano to be Kaiden. Seeing their father in front of me, brings back the pain I heard in

Kaiden's voice when he told me what the father did. I am not sure I can separate these two guys. I feel like this is some kind of cruel joke being played on me.

I look at Mr. and Mrs. Stagnitto. He sticks his hand out to shake mine, but I ignore it. I have no desire to touch him. I have no intention of getting to know him either. It makes me angry at him for what he did to Kaiden. I know in my head I shouldn't judge a person on someone else's opinion, but I can't help it. I love Kaiden and Gene hurt him deeply. How can Gaetano not be angry at his father for the lie he told him about Madeline being his real mother? How is he not pissed that Gene is the reason him and Kaiden don't have a relationship? I don't get it. Gaetano and Kaiden should be allowed to be brothers. If I had a sister or a brother, I'd want to know him or her.

They sit at our table. *"Ciara, our son has nothing but lovely words to say about you,"* Madeline says.

"Gaetano has been very kind to me."

Gene clears his throat. *"I have known your grandmother for many years."*

"Oh, really? Just how well do you two know each other?"

"We see each other quite often at charity events. Madeline and I have attended every New Year's Eve party since she started them."

"Yes, I put a bid in on that red dress you made. I was very disappointed I didn't win. It is a gorgeous dress, but I don't think I would have been as stunning as you were in it."

Once again, my mouth is on the floor. I have never met these people before, but yet, they have been in the house I grew up in. I lean over to Gaetano. *"I have to make a phone call. I'll be right back."* I see concern in his expression. *"If you'll excuse me, I have a phone call to make."* I feel like I can't breathe. This is all too much.

When I am far enough away from the crowd and the music, I open my contact list and dial Grams' number. She better answer.

"Ciara, how are you?"

"I am doing okay. We are at a cookout on the beach. I called to ask you a question."

"Okay, I'm listening."

"Did you know that Kaiden Marcellus and Gaetano Stagnitto are brothers?"

"What? How is that possible? I've known Stagnitto a long time. I think I would know if there was another child."

"Grams, they're not just brothers, but they are twins."

"I don't understand."

GRANDMA'S SILENT AUCTION

"The father raised Gaetano and didn't know about Kaiden. The mother never told Gene. Gaetano thought Madeline was his mother."

"Oh, dear! You know, I never once thought about how much the boys look alike. I'm sorry, Ciara, I never would've accepted both bids if I had known."

"I figured as much. I have to get back. For my own sanity, I had to ask."

"I love you."

"I love you, too."

I put my phone away and stay by myself a bit longer. I need to get my head back into knowing Gaetano. I am having a difficult time allowing him to shine through. He absolutely is trying to get to know me. I owe him the same.

I take a deep breath, I know I must go back. I just wish Gene wasn't here, though. I turn around to head back and Gaetano is standing there. He looks defeated.

"Is everything alright?"

"Yes, I just wanted to talk to Grams for a minute."

"I'm not going to lie, I overheard part of the conversation."

"I see."

"Listen, if you don't want to get to know my family, I'm not going to force that on you. I do hope

that you will still give me the chance to get to know you."

"I'm trying really hard to allow that."

"You love him, don't you?"

"We never said those words to each other."

"Doesn't mean you don't feel that way."

"If we are going to know each other, we cannot talk about my feelings for Kaiden or anyone else I have dated."

"Fair enough. What do I have to do to make you see only me when you look at me?"

"Just keep showing me who you are, I guess. I need to know you. I already see you have different personalities. I don't have all the answers."

"I really enjoyed the evening together. I'm sorry if I overstepped by inviting my family here. I just wanted you to see they are a big part of my life."

"I can understand that. I just wish I could have been warned."

"We don't have to go back. We can go for a walk or get a nightcap."

"A walk would be nice."

"Perfect."

GRANDMA'S SILENT AUCTION

We went for a very nice walk on the beach. Gaetano told me a few stories of him when he was a kid. His dance lessons and piano lessons. Both that he hated. He would have rather been outside riding a bike or playing with friends at the park. He said he lived a rich boy's lifestyle. He didn't care about money, he just wanted to be a kid. I laughed a few times when he told me things he would do to get out of the lessons. He was quite creative and a little rebellious. I wanted to tell him he and Kaiden were more alike as children than they probably know. I kept my mouth shut. This is about him. Not them.

We eventually called it a night. He dropped me off at my room, gave me a very nice kiss goodnight, then proceeded to his own room. I went inside, changed into pj shorts and a tank top. I was sitting on my bed processing the day when I opened Kaiden's email. I wonder if I should reply. I haven't done a very good job of cutting ties with any of the men. Maybe I should start doing that.

I get off my bed, wrap a blanket around my shoulders and go outside. I sit in a chair just outside my door. It is on the side closest to Gaetano's room. Nothing but lattice fencing separates our two areas.

My heart is telling me to respond to the email. My

brain is telling me to give it time before I do. I wish I knew which one I should listen to. I let out a puff of air and listen to the stronger voice. I open my email and type in his name in the address place.

Kaiden, words aren't always needed when the feelings out power them. I hear what you said. If we are meant to be, I hope you can handle the things I've done in the months before and after. - Ciara

I hit send and then I jump.

CHAPTER ELEVEN
GAETANO

It's been quite the morning and I haven't even been up that long. I woke to a knock at my door. The sun had barely shown its face. I rubbed my eyes with the heel of my hand as my father said good morning. I raised my brows wondering why he woke me from a perfectly beautiful dream at the ass crack of dawn. I let him into my room and he told me he and my mom were going home. I was surprised by his announcement. They just got here. Then he told me about a conversation he had with Ciara last night. I stared at him with disbelief. Seriously - he had the audacity to confront Ciara outside of our rooms. I was pissed! I said my goodbyes to him, covering the fact I was pissed. He left and I laid on the bed wanting to get more sleep. Yeah, that wasn't going to happen. I laid there rehashing his words. I wasn't just pissed at him, I was getting upset with Ciara as well. I have tried my damndest to be a man and overlook the fact she dated my brother so that we could get to know each other. It just keeps getting slapped in my face that he got to her first. I am done doing this. I don't want to compete with the brother I don't even know. It is clear that Ciara cares a great deal for Kaiden. People don't put my father in his place and she did. She did it without batting an eye.

I got off the bed and called the airline and booked a flight home. I leave later this afternoon. I was hoping it would be sooner, but there's nothing I can do about it. Well, I could charter a plane if I wanted to, but I see no reason to spend the ridiculous amount of money on one. If I were thinking clearly, I could have gone home with my family.

I packed my bags and waited in my room all morning. I was in no mood to see Ciara. I figured I could repay her and sneak away as she did to me. She'd probably even thank me for it.

I don't generally give up very easily when there is something I want. I'm not going to lie, I wanted her. I just see no need to continue to be nothing more to Ciara than my brother's lookalike. I didn't sign up for that. Honestly, it's getting exhausting. He won. Well, I at least hope he does in the end. Otherwise, I gave up too easily and neither one of us got the prize.

I wheel my luggage outside my doorstep and then go back inside because I forgot to leave a tip for maid service. I would have felt like shit if I didn't leave a tip. I feel horrible when I overhear my employees complain about it.

I step outside and face the door to lock the room up. *"Are you leaving?"*

Damn it, I was hoping she was gone or didn't come out of her room. *"Yes,"* I answer her.

"Oh!" I turn around and she is caught off guard by my leaving.

"I have a business to run. I can't stay here forever." I see she is dressed for sunbathing. *"Make sure you apply enough sunscreen this time."*

"I was coming to see if you wanted to join me at the pool."

"I would if I didn't have a flight to catch."

"Why are you really leaving?"

I am not a good liar. I have to tell her the truth. *"I spoke with my father this morning. He told me about the conversation you two had. My family is a big part of my life. It's clear you don't really like my father."* At least I didn't lie. What I said is true.

"I said my peace with him. So, do you want me to come back with you?"

"You don't have to do that. I have to go so that I don't miss my flight."

"You're throwing in the towel? Didn't think you were a quitter." She starts to walk away. *"Have a safe flight, Gaetano,"* she says over her shoulder.

I laugh - a quitter. I am definitely not one of those. Something else I am not is a fool. I grab the handle to my luggage and leave. The sooner I get back to Seven Jewels, the sooner I get my single life back. Hell, I may even find a lovely lady to fill my bed to get over her.

The shadow of my body blocks the sun from her eyes. *"I am not a quitter."*

Ciara lifts her sunglasses to peek at me. *"I didn't really believe you were. Did you miss your flight?"*

"I might have purposely missed it."

She gets up from the lounge chair. Fucking hell she is sexy in red! She drops her sunglasses on the lounge and steps past me. Her hand lightly brushing against mine. *"It's awfully hot, don't you think?"* Think - I know how hot it just got!

I turn and watch her dive into the pool. I didn't come back here to stand on the sidelines. I go to the pool and dive in after her. I caught her by the waist and pulled her toward me. *"It is very hot,"* I whisper in her ear. *"I can think of ways to make it even hotter."*

"Oh ya? How is that?"

I bring us to the edge of the pool and slide my hand down her torso and keep going lower. My fingers press against her clit. *"I want to give you an orgasm, right here and now."*

"There are people around."

"Who cares. They are at the other end and paying no attention to us."

"I don't know."

I move her bathing suit out of my way. I play with her clit. *"Don't moan or you'll give us away."* I enter my fingers inside her. *"I can see your nipples. I wish I could have them between my teeth."*

"Mmm."

"I would love to throw you up on the edge of the pool and taste you." I hook my fingers and I am rewarded with a soft moan. *"Your pussy is getting tighter around my fingers. Are you about to cum without my permission?"*

"No, sir." My cock throbs at the fact she called me sir.

"There is a man watching you intensely. I bet he knows you are going to orgasm. I'm sure he will go jerk off soon." She grabs my forearm. *"You are such a naughty girl. You like that he is getting hard and he can't have you. Cum on my fingers, Ciara."* She bites her thumb to hide her moan. Her pussy contracts. *"I need a drink."* I remove my fingers and swim away. If I don't get away from her, I'd fuck her right here. I seriously need a cold drink to cool off.

I keep my eye on Ciara swimming around. I also ordered both of us an icy mixed drink. I wasn't joking when I said it was hot out. Watching her just intensifies the scalding heat. I don't know what I was thinking this morning. I am glad I came to my senses and purposely missed my flight. I told myself I am no quitter, nor am I a fool. I would have been the biggest fool if I quit on her and our chance at love.

Ciara gets out of the pool. Despite the fact it is hot as fuck out here, her nipples are hard. I am surprised when she doesn't go to her own seat. Instead, she straddles my lap. She leans into my ear.

"I am glad you missed your flight."

She sits back up straight. *"So am I."* I lean

forward. *"You need to get off my lap. You are making my cock hard again."*

Ciara giggles. She inches forward and puts her pussy right over my erection. *"Is the old man staring at us?"*

I peek past her. *"Yep, and so is everyone else here."*

"I bet they would die if you fucked me right here."

"Should we go for it and see?"

Ciara leans to the side and picks up her drink. I groan when her pussy presses back against my manhood. She's not only putting on a little show for prying eyes, but she's teasing the fuck out of me. She'll pay for that later when we are in our room. I wonder if now would be a good time to tell her I lost my room?!

I am disappointed when she gets off my lap. *"I'm hungry. Are you going to take me to lunch?"*

"I'm sure I can manage that."

CHAPTER TWELVE
CIARA

Early this afternoon, I was a bit disappointed that Gaetano was leaving. He was about to sneak off as I did to him. My emotions have been on a rollercoaster ride for the past few days. I want to like Gaetano, but it has been difficult. After talking with Gene last night, I knew I had to start treating Gaetano as someone other than a man with Kaiden's face. He has been giving this relationship his all and I should give him the same. I told Gene that Kaiden isn't the same person as Gaetano, and now I need to separate them. I feel I let Gaetano down. I blame myself for him leaving. I can see he likes me.

I went to the pool as I was planning. I sat there baking in the sun thinking about whether or not I should chase after him. Ever since meeting Gaetano, I have been so damn confused. I already had enough on my plate with feelings for other men and then I got this thrown in my lap. One minute I want to give him a chance then the next, I was relieved he was basically letting me off the hook. I just don't know what the right thing to do is. Being in Jamaica has been nice. However, it might be time I go home. Take the next two and a half weeks to get my head on straight.

I was in shock when he came back. I think that took a lot of guts. It also really showed me he isn't a quitter. Nobody wants to be with a man that is a quitter if a challenge approaches. At least I don't.

I got off of his lap. What he did to me in the pool was hot. I wanted to tease him a little in return, but I am still unsure how far we should go with a sexual relationship. I think we need to establish who we are before we take things further. I wasn't lying when I told him it hurt to be called a slut. I kind of want to take a step back. I can have relationships with these men without being in their beds.

I pushed the thought of sex out of my mind and asked Gaetano to feed me. I am hungry but I could have waited longer to eat. It was more of an excuse than anything. I had to put distance between our bodies. We walked to the hut that we had dinner at a couple of nights ago. The girl, Erica, isn't working. We ordered something light to eat. We start talking about nothing too important. Then I brought up the idea that we go back to Vegas. I told him I wanted to see him in his element. He seems okay with it. He did get on his phone to rebook his flight and got me a ticket as well. Our seats are not next to each other, but at least we are both leaving at the same time.

Gaetano asked me what I would like to do since we are leaving bright and early in the morning. I told him to surprise me. We ate our lunch in silence as he was busy making plans for our last day here. I am very curious about what he is planning since he wouldn't as much as even give me a hint.

I heard my phone chime. As much as I wanted to see who it was, I didn't look. I'm trying to give Gaetano my full attention.

"You should see who that is. Last time you ignored your phone it was important."

I dug my phone out of my tote bag. I saw that it was Malcolm. He sent me a text telling me he was back in the States. I didn't reply. It wasn't urgent. I can send him a text later when I'm alone in my room later.

"Nope, not important." I put it back in my purse to show him it's not.

"Are you ready for an adventure."

"Let's do it. I am excited to see what is in store."

Gaetano pays the bill and then we leave. We take the path to the front of the resort where a Jeep is waiting for us. We get in and he takes off with a led foot. The wind blowing against my face feels good. Gaetano seems to be enjoying the ride, too, with his hair blowing in all sorts of directions. His smile is contagious.

We get to where he is taking me after a lot of turns and hilly roads. We have gone into a heavily wooded area where he parks the Jeep. I look around and wish I had something other than flip flops on. It looks as if we are going hiking. We get out and meet at the front of the Jeep.

"I'm not sure I'm dressed right for this."

His eyes travel over my body. *"Oh, I think you are."*

Gaetano takes my hand and we begin to walk toward a path. I am relieved it is a clean path. It's not stone or paved, but at least it is clean dirt. We keep going further into the woods. I am not going to lie, I'm a little frightened. This is out of my comfort zone.

It has probably been a good mile walk. We reach a large opening. I smile at the sound of a waterfall. We walk to a metal railing. It's a deep drop if someone were to fall.

He points out the waterfall. *"That's where we are going."*

"How do we get there?"

"I'll show you."

We turn and we go to another area. I inhale and hold my breath. *"I am not crossing that."* I turn back to get the hell outta here. I don't do heights. Especially, when my feet aren't on solid ground.

Gaetano comes to be in front of me. Walking backward as he says, *"I'll be with you every step of the way."*

"I can't do it. It's making me nauseous just thinking about it."

"How about we try this, I'll go in front of you to guide you and you keep your eyes closed."

"That won't work. I already know about the rope bridge."

"It will work. You won't even know when we start to cross."

"Can't we drive to the other side?"

"This is the only way." Gaetano's hands cup my face. *"I'd never put your life in danger."*

"I know."

I squeeze my eyes shut so tightly that it almost hurts. I peek one eye open as he guides me around. We haven't left solid ground yet. *"I saw this beautiful woman walk into my hotel and my heart skipped a few beats. The natural beauty of this woman is pure. All I wanted to do at the moment was to talk to her. My curiosity was off the charts. Why was this woman alone? Would she even talk to me if I approached her? I knew she was here early. She wasn't in my hotel for me. I sure wished she were. I hated that I couldn't go to her and sweep her off her feet. I was saddened by the fact I had to wait. Waiting isn't my strong point. When I want something, I don't wait. I go for it and don't quit until it's mine. I am learning patience. Sometimes something so beautiful is worth the wait."*

We stop moving. His hands hold my face. I can feel the warmth of his presence as his mouth comes closer to mine. I open my eyes briefly before he kisses me. The soft kiss is filled with a gentleness. I know this man is falling for me. I am not there yet, but I can tell my guard is fading away. Maybe there can be something between us.

"You made it."

"Thanks to you."

He gives me another peck on the lips before taking me and tugging me along. I see him. I think I finally see Gaetano and not Kaiden.

CHAPTER THIRTEEN
GAETANO

The way I lead Ciara across the bridge is something I've never done for a woman before. I never cared enough about a woman's feelings to get that involved. If this were any other woman, I would not have cared about her fears or have been that sensitive. I would have crossed the bridge alone and said come if you're coming if not wait in the car. To me it has never mattered if a woman liked me outside the bedroom or not. That's mostly what women were for me - sex. Ciara is different. She makes me want more than sex. I find myself changing for the better. She makes me want more out of life than my hotel, casino, and the occasional one-night stand. I want a real relationship and I want to be with her. I hope she felt it in the kiss.

When we reach the waterfall. *"Last one in has to buy dinner."*

I strip my shirt off as Ciara takes her little skirt wrap off. She slips her shoes off quicker than I can. Before I know it, she's diving into the water. I hurry and get mine off. I dive in and come up. I then swim to where she is treading water.

"Looks like dinner is on you."

"I'm good with that."

I bring her to me and she wraps her legs around my waist. She bends backward, letting her upper body float. I rub my hand over her breast. My manhood twitches as I feel her nipple beneath my palm. She watches my eyes as I slide my hand into her suit. Her eyes close when I pinch her nipple. She then sits up, putting her arms around my neck. Her lips meet mine. I get a hold of the straps of her bathing suit and bring them past her shoulders. She lets go long enough for me to get the straps past her arms. I lean her upper body back into the water. Her breasts are beautiful. Her legs untangle from my waist as I get her suit fully off.

"Take yours off too."

I take my trunks off and swim them to land. I turn to see where she's gone. I spot her swimming toward the falls. I swim out to where she's at. It is more shallow. I stand and the water only comes to my waist. I watch Ciara stand and walk into the falls. I started to go to her as she disappeared. I stop in my tracks when I see her sitting on a little hidden rock bed. Man, I want to devour her. I want to sexually please her to a point I ruin her for all other men. Only my hands and my cock can satisfy her.

I pull Ciara so that her ass is to the edge. I spread her legs apart. I lean in and lick her lower lips. My mouth waters for more. I dip my tongue into her pussy. Her fingers comb through my hair. My cock hardens the more I taste her sweet juice. I bring my hand up to her clit, she fists my hair as I pinch it. A moan echoes as it bounces off the rocks.

I move my mouth to her lower body and kiss her just above the belly button. I move again but this time I kiss her mouth. I give her my tongue with the lingering flavor of her pussy. My cock is throbbing and begging to be inside her. I'm not done getting my fill of her on my tongue. So, I work my way back down her body, sucking on her nipples before I lick her and suck her clit between my lips. I use my fingers to bring her to an orgasm, then I lick it all up.

I position myself between her legs, ready for my cock to fill her. She gets up before I can penetrate her. I watch her kneeling before me. She strokes my shaft and cups my balls. I throw my head back as she licks the smooth skin of the head. She licks the entire length and back up. I groan as she wraps her lips around the girth and slides her mouth down. My cock disappears into her mouth. I groan again as her mouth fucks my cock. I feel my balls rise as the orgasm nears. I tried to pull out but she grabbed my ass, dug her fingers into the skin. I open my mouth to tell her I'm going to cum. I can't get the words out as she takes me fully in. I cum in her throat. Fuck, it felt spectacular. Before I can do anything else, Ciara goes running off. I watch her dive back into the water when it gets deep enough. I just stand here and watch. I am a little confused as to what just happened. Oral sex is great, but it was meant as foreplay.

I eventually get my head out of my ass and swim out to where she is swimming around. She is playful when she splashes my face with water. We mess around for quite some time before we get out to get dressed. I could stay here all day with her.

We sat for a while and she told me about her childhood. Then we decided to get heading back. I had to guide her back across the rope bridge. This time she trusted me enough that she opened her eyes halfway through. Today turned out to be the best. I am almost sad that I won't have her to myself once we leave in the morning to go back to Vegas. On a good note, she's still mine for a couple more weeks. I'm going to make it the best couple weeks possible. I don't want this woman to forget me.

We get back to the resort and go to her room. She was cool about the fact I no longer had a room here. She said I could stay with her as long as I slept on the floor. I hope that was just a joke. I guess I'll find out later.

We both take showers and put on fresh clothes. I am letting her pick where we are going to dinner. I see her checking for places on her phone. She seems to be happy that I came back. I know I am. I think we are finally on our way to having a good relationship.

CHAPTER FOURTEEN
CIARA

I didn't make Gaetano sleep on the floor on our last night in Jamaica. By the time we went to bed, we called it a night. We both knew we had to be up early to be at the airport. I cozied up next to him and we both fell asleep.

Once we returned to Vegas, I went to the room I had and gathered up my stuff to move to the penthouse suite to be with him. For the last couple of weeks, I've been sleeping in his bed. Even though Gaetano and I have become closer, we haven't had sex. I mean nothing more than oral sex. I told him I just wasn't ready to cross that line. He seemed fine with respecting my wishes. I am having a difficult time figuring out if I didn't want to cross that line because of Kaiden or if I am more worried about the past relationships I have already had and the future ones. It deeply bothers me to be called a slut. Before this experience, my body count wasn't that high.

Just because Gaetano and I didn't have intercourse doesn't mean he is out of the running. I have spent just about every second of the day with him. I have learned things about him that I don't believe any other women in his past know. The things about him outside the bedroom. I learned that he can tease a girl and leave them wanting more. I did want more. Let me tell you, he showed me enough of him to know, he likes to be in control. He is a dominant through and through. Probably because he is in control, it stopped us from crossing that line.

In the last couple of weeks, we talked about how he feels cheated about not having a relationship with Kaiden. A few times, I was tempted to call Kaiden to get him to come to Seven Jewels so that I could lock the two stubborn asses in a room. As much as I would love for the two of them to mend fences, it's not my place to fix that for them. That's something they must do on their own. If it were to happen, I think Gaetano would be the first to break. Not because he is the weaker man, but because he is such a family man. He talked about his family a lot. Kaiden is used to being alone and hasn't had anyone since his mom passed away.

Tonight is the last night I'll be with Gaetano. I have a flight in the morning to go home. I am looking forward to spending a few days at home with Alaska before I have to run off somewhere else to be with another man. I can't wait to go out to dinner with Porter. Maybe I can see Grams too. I miss them both dearly.

"You look stunning, Ms. Verbank."

I spin around and walk toward Gaetano who is standing in the doorway. *"You don't look too shabby yourself, Mr. Stagnitto."*

"I want to thank you in advance for tonight. I know you don't care too much for my father."

I put my finger to his lips. *"You don't have to thank me. I'm doing it for you not me. I care about what makes you happy."*

"Maybe tonight he'll change your opinion of him."

I highly doubt that. I wrap my arms around his waist and I smile, then kiss his cheek. *"Maybe."*

He kisses me on the forehead before we head out. We are going to Gene and Madeline's home for dinner. I'm not really keen on the idea, but it is what it is. It's that whole compromise thing you do for a relationship. I didn't promise to be on my best behavior, however, I'm going to give it my best shot.

It took almost an hour to get to the Stagnitto's home. I didn't realize that they lived this far away. For some reason I thought they lived closer to the strip. When we pulled up there was a butler waiting at the door for us. He let us in and led us to a large family room.

"This place is gorgeous. Did you grow up here?"
"I did."

I realize now that Gaetano grew up with money. I have no idea what Gene did for a living or how this family became this rich. This home is a mansion. It reminds me of Grams' in many ways. I know my grandma worked her ass off to get where she was. The MV clothing line has a lot of blood, sweat, and tears. I wonder if Gene had become rich the same way. Maybe he married money. It could very well be Madeline was the breadwinner and Gene got lucky.

I glance at Gaetano. Do I have the right to ask? I can't help it when I think about Ms. Marcellus. She probably never had a fighting chance to keep both boys. She was poor. I walk around the room looking at stuff. I cannot let Gaetano question me on what I'm thinking. This is our last night together. I have to remain focused on him. He's the one I'm dating. It isn't my place to butt my nose in where it doesn't belong.

Gaetano comes up behind me, putting his hands on my waist. He kisses the back of my head. *"It's just a house."*

I spin around. I touch his cheek, my fingers combing through his beard. I smile. *"I know. I grew up in one just like it."*

"So, you know this place doesn't define who I am, right?"

"There's a little bit of false in that statement. You grew up in a loving home with people who love and support you. There's nothing wrong with that. What happened in these walls shaped you to be the person you are. So, it does in a way define you. The person I know isn't a rich snob and doesn't throw it in people's faces that you have money. That's because you decided to be a kind and caring person. We are alike in the way we grew up. Large home, money in our pockets, and never had to worry. So what that we come from money. Being rich does define us, we just choose not to flaunt it."

"Did I tell you that I still took the bus to school for three months after my parents bought me a brand new Lexus. I didn't want to be a show-off. It was just a car to me, but to my friends it would have been

rubbing it in their face just how rich my parents were."

"You had us trade it in for a used car so that you could stop taking the bus."

We both turn to see Gene and Madeline behind us. Gaetano goes to them. He hugged and kissed both of them on the cheek. Madeline came to me and gave me a hug. Gene kept his distance. Which I was fine with.

Madeline offers us a drink while we wait for dinner to be served. We all sit and I sip my wine. Gaetano tells his parents how we went to the casino the other night and jokes how I was sucking him dry with the amount of money I was winning on the roulette table. I joked back that I gave it all back at the blackjack table and said the cards were stacked against me.

The maid came to the room to tell us that dinner is ready to be served. I walked beside Gaetano with his hand on my lower back. He was a gentleman when he pulled my seat out for me. I witnessed Gene doing the same with Madeline. Manners are a good quality to have .

Dinner was a big Italian menu. I have to admit, the food was incredible. Gene told me that the recipes have been in his family for generations. I learned that his parents came to America right before he was born.

After we eat dinner we go outside to the back patio. We have more wine. Madeline asked Gaetano for help inside, leaving me alone with Gene. I was hoping that wouldn't happen. I was tempted to get up and follow Gaetano into the house.

"Take a walk with me, Ms. Verbank."

That didn't sound like a question. It was a demand. I didn't want to go. *"Sure."* I pick up my wine glass and bring it with me.

I walk next to Gene but keep my distance. He isn't talking and I'm sure not going to be the one to open my mouth. We reach the end of the path and Gene flicks a switch on a pole. He points out into the distance. I see lights on in what looks like a treehouse.

"Gaetano was five when I had that built for him. Madeline and I had trouble getting our son out of it. Warm summer nights, he would sneak out here and sleep in it. He never stopped going in it until he moved out."

"That's a nice story. Thanks for sharing it with me."

"I have thought a lot about our conversation in Jamaica. I have been trying to figure out the best way

to make amends with Kaiden. If I had known about him, I would have been a good father to him. He would have been in that treehouse with his brother or I would have found what he loved. I am not a bad man. I love Gaetano very much."

"If you would have known about him you would have taken him, too, is what you mean. I have no doubt you would have loved Kaiden and given him a good life. It's clear you are a good father. It's not really my business about what happened."

"You have established an opinion of me. I did what I thought was best for my boy. I was with Madeline by the time I found Janie was pregnant. My parents pushed for me to get custody. Janie was in no shape to raise a child."

"But maybe if you never took Ms. Marcellus to court, you both would have been parents to both children. You had the money to support her and the boys."

"I wasn't keeping Gaetano from her. It was set up for her to have visitation. She turned it down. Said it would be too difficult. It's not hard to figure out now that she turned it down because she knew she was pregnant with twins. It was her plan to separate the boys and also separate from me as well."

"Listen, Gene, what happened was a very long

time ago. It's sick and twisted. Janie and you both had a hand in that. Again, it isn't really my business. I only have an opinion because Kaiden means a lot to me. He no longer has a family. He had nobody since he lost his mother until me, and now, he doesn't even have that. He felt rejected by you. If you want to know your son, you are the one that has to fix that, not me. Other than that one flaw, I think you are a good person. I came here tonight for Gaetano. I didn't come here for you to prove that you love Gaetano and that you would have loved Kaiden if you knew about him. Guess what, Gene, you know about him, so go love him and be a father."

"Putting my father in his place again, I see."

Goddamn it! I spin on my heels. I didn't want this to happen again. *"I didn't start this, he did. Your treehouse seems lovely."*

I walk away because frankly, I am embarrassed that conversation happened. I feel horrible about the expression on Gaetano's face. I hurt him. It wasn't intentional, but I still hurt him.

I walked back into the house and kept going for the front door. The butler sees me coming and he opens it for me. I go out to the car and get in. I want to get the hell out of here.

The passenger door flies open. *"Ciara, come back inside."*

"Not happening."

"You know I'm not mad at you, right? A lot of what you said makes sense."

"I didn't come here for him. I didn't want to have that conversation with him either."

"I know that."

"Can you please take me back to your hotel? I'm tired and I still need to pack."

"You cannot even look at me right now, can you?" I shake my head no. I am too upset, pissed, and embarrassed. *"I'll have the driver take you back. I'm going to stay here tonight."*

"You're breaking up with me?"

"We have to do that in a few hours anyway. This will be easier on us both."

"Really? It's best to break up on a bad note. Gotcha."

"Again, Ciara, I'm not mad at you. Someone had to spell it out to him that if he never took my biological mother to court, I'd have known my mother. Honestly, I'm staying here because I don't want to watch you pack your bags. I am crazy about you. I never want you to leave." He turns my head to look at

him. *"I was planning on staying here tonight long before that conversation."*

"I'm so sorry. I really tried to keep my mouth shut."

Gaetano leans in the car and shuts me up by kissing me. *"I'd ask you to marry me the moment you stepped foot in my hotel if I could have. You know I'll be waiting for you in the same place you first saw me."*

He kisses me again then shuts the door. I don't know when a driver got in the car, but it starts moving before I do anything. What the hell just happened? Why the hell did our last night together end like this?

When I arrive back at the hotel alone, I go up to the penthouse suite and pack my bags. I don't know where I'm going, but I am not staying here tonight. Maybe I can catch an earlier flight home. I sure as hell can't wait to get there. I am maxed out on the drama. I am done trying to balance my feelings.

I pick up my phone to call the airlines and cross my fingers there's an earlier flight. I see I have a new email. I open it and read it. I send back a reply then call the airlines. I smile. I got an earlier flight by six hours. I still have time to blow. I finish packing and leave. *"Goodbye, Gaetano,"* I say to an empty room.

ABOUT THE AUTHOR

Thank you so much for taking the time to read Grandma's Silent Auction May. Word-of-mouth is crucial for any author to succeed. If you enjoyed the book, please leave a review on Amazon. Even if it's just a sentence or two. It would make all the difference and would be very much appreciated. – OXOX Michael James

Website: http://michaeljames-author332.bravesites.com/

ALSO BY MICHAEL JAMES

If you enjoyed Grandma's Silent Auction May, you may also like my other books:

The Way We Love series:

Pink Skies At Night

Shadows At Night

Nights Are Unlimited

Concealed By The Night

Shattered At Night

Freed At Night

Winning A Cowgirl's Heart - Trilogy:

The Rodeo King

The Best Friend

The Fate Of My Heart

Winning a Cowgirl's Heart -Complete Box Set

Construction Vs. Corporate- Trilogy:

Unbalanced

Balancing

Balanced

Secrets Within a Club

Club Comrade

Revenge

Saving Club Conrad

Masquerade Saga

His Pearls

His Secrets

His Prison

His Games

His Moves

All His

Crime in Landkaster series

The Mirror

Times Like These

Lonely Road of Faith

Grandma's Silent Auction series

January

February

March

April

Standalone:

Toying With October

Pieces Of Me

A Christmas For Eve

Dom Diaries: Tangled Up In You

Christmas Scavenger Hunt

Blue Christmas

Stealing the Christmas Spotlight

Co-written with Jodi Fahey

Last Sheet

Manufactured by Amazon.ca
Bolton, ON

44213037R00059